El Tigre /
Juan Darien

E. Thomalen

A Samuel French Acting Edition

FOUNDED 1830

SAMUELFRENCH.COM
SAMUELFRENCH-LONDON.CO.UK

FOR PRODUCTION ENQUIRIES

UNITED STATES AND CANADA
Info@SamuelFrench.com
1-866-598-8449

UNITED KINGDOM AND EUROPE
Theatre@SamuelFrench-London.co.uk
020-7255-4302

Each title is subject to availability from Samuel French, depending upon country of performance. Please be aware that *EL TIGRE / JUAN DARIEN* may not be licensed by Samuel French in your territory. Professional and amateur producers should contact the nearest Samuel French office or licensing partner to verify availability.

EL TIGRE / JUAN DARIEN was first produced by Hip Pocket Theatre at The University of Texas at Arlington Theatre Arts Program on December 1, 2001. The performance was directed by Diane Simons, with sets by Lake Simons, costumes by Diane Simons, lighting by Michael Garner and musical direction by Brandon Brown. The cast was as follows:

STUDENT/CHILD/MS. JAGUAR . . . . .Lori Fox

THE MAYOR . . . . Shawn Gann

JUAN DARIEN . . . . .Jonathan Hernandez

THE ANIMAL TRAINER . . . . .Brad Hughes

MOTHER . . . . Lisa James

PALLBEARER . . . . Jason Kendall

KNIFE THROWER/MR. BONES . . . . Paul Logsdon

CIRCUS BARKER . . . . Mike Murray

TRAPEZE ARTIST . . . . Nicole Murphy

SNAKE . . . . Dennis O'Neill

HUNTER . . . . .Gustavo Valentin

TEACHER . . . . .William Whitehead

STUDENT/CHILD/CIRCUS TROUPE MEMBER/MR. JAGUAR . . .Billy Wise

CHILDREN . . . . Erika Bustamate, Melissa Hurta

STUDENTS . . . . .Aja Jones, Emmy Zabcik

CIRCUS TROUPE MEMBERS . . . . .Jodi Ganshirt, Kristen Hudson,
Kerri Montagnino

MUSICIANS . . . . Brandon Brown, Joe Stencel

CHARACTERS

(in order of appearance)

STORYTELLER

MR. JAGUAR

MS. JAGUAR

(KIT)JUAN DARIEN

HUNTER

MOTHER

SNAKE

TEACHER

STUDENT 1

STUDENT 2

STUDENT 3

STUDENT 4

PALLBEARER

CIRCUS BARKER

TRAPEZE ARTIST

KNIFE THROWER

ANIMAL TRAINER

MAYOR

CHILD 1

CHILD 2

Non Speaking Characters include: Pilgrim, Mr. Bones (Death), Grandmother, Grandfather, Milk Maid, Farmer, Herdsman, Priest, Bride and Groom, Altar boy, Nursing Mother, Students, Townspeople, Tigers, etc.

Doubling is possible for many speaking and non-speaking roles.

AUTHOR'S NOTES

The text for this work is but the skeleton upon which the work is co-constructed by the performers in a sense more than is true of most plays. Building it out requires music, choreography, magic and masque. It is also an ensemble piece. The lines of the STORYTELLER are delivered by the ensemble: not as a chorus, but individually, by different actors (except for the first five and last four which should be delivered by the same actor). The music may be improvisational, there are many good musicians who can work this way, and who can share in the creation of a work for the stage. The musical style may be Latin, jazz/blues, rock, or even the otherworldly Andean flute music. Dance is important to telling the story, and will depend upon the style of the music. The story should be enacted in dance, e.g., in the sequence of death taking off souls of the village, in the jaguar's courting scene, in the school scene, in death taking Mother's soul, in the mourner's scene, in the circus scene, etc. The play is meant to run about 75 minutes.

*To Diane Simons, a truly extraordinary artist, who was the first to
bring this work to life on the stage and whose artistic vision has set the
standard for all future productions of this work.
She has set a high standard indeed!*

E. Thomalen

(A man sits with his back against an adobe wall and a sombrero is tilted down over his eyes. Suddenly he appears to waken, agitated. He addresses the audience.)

STORYTELLER. Stop…Senor and listen, *Por favor!*
From dreams have I now found release, or
Am I caught in these illusions yet?
Permit me to recount what I have spied,
Then you, the matter, will decide.
I wandered through a jungle some,
And came upon a town beset,
With melancholy groans from
Every house and church and public square,
For an appalling plague had struck them there,
And so affected, many villagers have died.

*(**MR. BONES** appears and dances with the old man and woman and each character mentioned)*

Death carried off the nodding pair,
The grandmother and grandfather,
Who smoothed their grandchild's hair.
Yes, and it struck the milk maid, too;
And, taking from that death a cue,
It struck the cow and chicken too.
The maize no longer felt the hoe,
For even the farmer was laid low.
Nor did the herdsman, or the herd, survive
Nor was the priest left long alive.
The fortune of the bride and groom
Was but a short-lived honeymoon;
An uninvited specter at the feast
Left not until his palm was creased

With a grave, *pestilential*, trist.
Nor was the mewling infant spared,
Nor altar boy uniquely fared.
The nursing mother's milk went dry,
No longer hearing the new baby's cry.
And when the bitter plague was done,
When all were dead, or fled, save one,
Who still remained within her home;
The jungle, then, o'er grew the town.
But who was left alive of all
That once had lived there, great and small?
It was a woman, childless now,
Without a husband, horse, or cow.
And every day she cut a flower,
Hoping to receive its power.
Though never did she bloom like it!
For after the plague's fury hit,
She could no longer that grief quit.
While all around the fecund jungle lay,
And in its fronds the beasts did play!

MR. JAGUAR. Come my pretty, come with me!

MS. JAGUAR. Oh Sir, where are you *taking* me?

MR. JAGUAR. Far from the lonely sadness of the loon,
To the *intoxicating* gardens of the moon!

MS. JAGUAR. For *sure* that is a spot that's rare!
We can enjoy our revels there!

MR. JAGUAR. I will give you sweet pleasure and a kit
And you shall evermore remember it!

(*They go off.*)

STORYTELLER. And so a Jaguar cub was born,
Betimes, upon a winter's morn.
Into a world both lush, and green,
Into a world that hummed unseen.
And pleased was he, this master, small,

With Mother there at every call!
But to the rich and verdant spot
A hunter came with gun and shot,
Just looking for an ornamental thing,
A bird, or snake, or jaguar skin.

HUNTER. This bird's bright feather will make a fine hat.
I am certain of that!
And this serpent's shiny scales
Will certainly enhance my sales!
But still, a jaguar fur's a prize
That can make any buyer rise
And seize it, quickly, if he's wise!

STORYTELLER. The Hunter waited, silent as the trees,
And listened to the sound on every breeze.
He listened for the low and carefree growl,
Looked for the jaguar's tawny cowl,
Arising from the dappled jungle floor,
Arising to drink, or to eat, once more.
But at that special, clanging hour
Did all the animals begin to cower,
Except man, trusting to the rifle's power,
Rose, and looking grim and dour,
Destroyed the jewel of nature's bower.
And when he came upon his kill,
There lying in its warm blood still,
His eyes alight with gory thrill
For hunting was his only skill,
Then had he not yet *all* his fill!
Examining what he had shot,
He knew that this mother was not
Alone, but had a kit with her.
And so he listened, yet once more,
To see whether the kit might stir,
And he obtain another fur.

But the kit had perceived the power
Of the hunter, and the rifles glower,
So it was still, as sunshine in that hour,
Before the dark, before the show'r.
The hunter looked then to detect the track,
But dusk had fallen, and night was black.
And the kit, with its Mother dead,
Having waited out the hunter, fled.
Yet having left that dreadful scene,
The kit no longer knew where it had been,
Nor where it was, nor what had seen.
All its firm sinews now were slack,
And in its head there was a clack.
It only felt its hunger keen,
And hoped for something not too mean,
To fill its stomach, calm its spleen,
Against its terrors form a screen.
And in this very jumbled state,
It came upon a garden gate;
And there, at first, did hesitate;
Should it turn back, or pass, and separate,
From all it had known of the wild estate.
And so it paused, and so it stood,
Yet undecided what it would.
But, there, both weak and desperate,
It trusted to its hidden fate,
Whether to refuge find or counterfeit;
And pushed through the unlocked and unclosed gate,
Just as the childless Mother's dark mood
Made her come out for a spate
Of walking, and to ruminate
On her own child's unkind fate.
So it was the unlikely pair
Met in the evening's troubled air.

MOTHER. I see you have a fearsome form,
Yet do not take from me alarm
For I can see that you need balm,
Against the grief, against the harm.
Come, frightened kit, here to my arm!

STORYTELLER. And come it did, at her behest.
And come it did, to find a rest.
And in its hunger, it was blest;
For when she brought it to her shriveled breast,
It bloomed just like the flower of her quest!
And never was there such a guest,
Thus welcomed with so great a zest,
And through the night it did attest
To the healing power her love possessed.
But when the light of early day
Shot out its dart, its glinting ray,
Then went the hunter to repay,
A visit to the spot where he had slain
The jaguar Mother yesterday!
And he looked for the broken lay
Of the grass, and the marks on the clay,
That told him of the kit's pathway.

HUNTER. How could I let him get away?
Am I, here, losing my cachet?
Can man be losing natural sway
O'er animals that roar and bray?
This kit will not escape me yet,
About that there's no need to fret.
I will not be denied my kill!
Why, if the truth is known, it's whet
My appetite to get him still!
Upon it, now, my heart is set!

STORYTELLER. The hunter followed close the track
By using all his craft and knack.

The kit's trail led him to a shack,
A house, with gate ajar but still a crack,
And, there, he paused taken aback.
For the footprints stopped on a pack
An earthen plinth next to the door
He saw something he'd not seen before
No prints beyond it, to the back.
So stepping to the door, he gave a knock.
The mood of those inside was shock!
Without response, impatient, still another sock!

MOTHER. I do refuse to care for you in vain.
I shall not give up to death, one
Whom I have loved like this, again.
I cannot, more, endure such pain!
If in His wisdom, God will have it done;
Then I release you from this plain,
Of human habitation's gain.
Return to where you were begun!
I would not see your birth undone.

(takes the kit to the back door when a **SNAKE** *appears and startles her)*

SNAKE. Stop, Mother, do not my shape despise,
For in this form, this strange disguise,
As a snake, I, here, materialize.
I come to help you, and advise
How you may give the Hunter a surprise.

MOTHER. How strange, Sir, to hear a snake speak!
How strange to find a snake play hide and seek!

SNAKE. I associate with you because you're wise;
That lives have equal value you surmise.
I gave to you this kit in your deep sorrow,
And see how it's changed you on the morrow.
Put him in your loose rebozo,
Do not fear the Hunter's braggadocio.

Do not fear the Hunter's evil shadow
He shall never take what I bestow.

STORYTELLER. The Mother did as she was told.
She guessed the snake on her threshold
Must be enchanted, and quite old.
As swiftly as he did appear,
That swiftly did he disappear.
She turned to face the Hunter near,
Not knowing whether she'd prevail
Or he take from her what she held dear;
There take from her what she did fear.

MOTHER. Sir! Please don't continue on like that!
This is a humble hearth and home,
I put out a cordial "Welcome"!
I am not an aristocrat!
But courteous to all who do appear
Before my door, and wish to have my ear!
Accept from me such greetings here!

HUNTER. Please…I am looking, Madame, for the *cat!*

MOTHER. The cat? Pray tell me, Sir, *what* cat?

HUNTER. Ah…Madame, do not fool with me!
I ask you only where it's at!

MOTHER. I haven't it, as you can see.

HUNTER. When hunting yesterday, I shot
A jaguar in a wooded spot;
And, while examining her, I saw she'd begot
A kit, and still suckled the tot.
But, nowhere could I find the lot
Of him, before night rendered all obscure!
Today, when I meant the pelt to secure,
I followed his path, very sure
'Til it lead here; and my conjecture
Is here I'll find the answer!

MOTHER. Sir, you may search all through my house,
But I have no such refugee.

Besides, a jaguar kit is surely risky,
And the thought of it is simply ludicrous.
It makes me wonder: What's your purpose?
Do you task me because I have no spouse?
Or, is this the low humor of a souse?

HUNTER. I've tracked him to your door,
So I ask you to step aside, withdraw;
For I insist that I explore
And I shall find that jaguar;
On that you may set store!
You, Madame, for me hold no allure!
I am here only to complete a chore.

MOTHER. Then, Sir, proceed if it's your will,
I have no power to keep you from your fill.
Still, Sir, think what it is that you'd kill!

(*The* HUNTER *searches through the house and finding
nothing comes back and points with his gun at the*
MOTHER*'s shawl.*)

HUNTER. I have now searched both high and low,
And here are you the while abiding!
So I return to you my lady!
I must ask you to open your *rebozo,*
So I can more clearly see and know,
And tell if you are hiding
Something that has made it grow!
Don't try me further with bravado!

STORYTELLER. Then did she think her love was lost.
And hard upon her fell a frost;
Her spirit could not bear the cost;
Life's path could not be further crossed.
So, with a hopeless tug, the cloth was tossed.
But at that moment came a flash of fire
That even stilled the hunter's ire,
And caused the senses to retire.

And on returning to the scene
Caused the dazed Hunter to misfire;
Caused the awed Mother to admire,
What the great power of the Snake
Had made, there, to transpire.
Upon her hip was a small infant to attire.

HUNTER. Excuse me, Madame, but I did not know
That you had a young Michael Angelo.
It's clear the kit is not here, I'll go.

STORYTELLER. The Mother was filled with joy,
At her new baby boy;
When through the door slipped the sleek envoy
That had foretold her new employ,
Now to remind her that human fate's an alloy,
Of one's love, with grief that can destroy.

SNAKE. Now, Mother, do you recognize this son?
This stranger has become Juan Darien!
Though to your species he is alien,
For he is of a feline chorion,
Still you shall civilize and shapen,
And transform his rude essence.
As long as man treats him with fairness,
He shall be man's friend, and fearless;
But if treated as base, wild and worthless
He will forsake all that's human!

STORYTELLER. But so rapt was the Mother in her bliss,
So eager to bestow kiss after kiss
On the child's brow, that she did miss
The warning in the snake's hiss,
Spoken as with a strange awareness.

MOTHER. *(She turns away from the audience.)*
How soon you do walk!
How soon you do talk!
Too soon do you balk

    At your fond Mother's urgings
    My dear little sparrow hawk!
    Still you must learn to use a spoon
    And use a fork, and then pencil and chalk!
    No more can you stalk
    In the jungle, but soon
    Must stride on the sidewalk.

STORYTELLER. And in time he grew to school age,
    And his Mother took him to engage
    In writing, and in reading from the page,
    With others all at the same stage.
    And teachers thought him smart by their gauge.
    Juan thought, at times, it was but a cage!

TEACHER. Now, students, please come to attention!
    Why you balk defies all comprehension!
    Or, perhaps, for education, there are none
    If it requires some serious exertion!
    Must I the ruler take for coercion?
    School is not just a diversion!
    Let's start up today with a subtraction!
    If you start with two, take away one,
    What is the result of the transaction?
    Juan Darien?

JUAN DARIEN. Sir, it is but an orphan!

TEACHER. Once again you've proved a skillful marksman
    By so taking sure aim at my question!
    Tell me children, I'm asking:
    Of all that you know, who is king
    Of this lush and green mountain ring?

STUDENT 1. Why Sir, it's the men ruling
    The village to which we so fearfully cling!

STUDENT 2. Not so, it is the woman baking
    The bread and bearing the nursling!

STUDENT 3. Oh no, it's not that, but the princeling

In Spain, who holds us fast on a string!

STUDENT 4. For those who are church going,
It's the priest whose word is guiding.

TEACHER. Juan Darien you have sat there unblinking
Have you no views on this thing?

JUAN DARIEN. Sir, it's not man here that is king!

TEACHER. My boy, what are you thinking?

JUAN DARIEN. Why it's all that are now living
At the edge of this small man-made clearing.
For man thinks he is the master at the meeting,
Yet mast'ry is nothing, if not fleeting.
And when man leaves with his gun, and with his Gatling,
The jaguar again by cunning,
And by claw, shall conquer and be ruling.

STORYTELLER. So it was, the young man had thus answered
Without fear, and wholly free, and quite uncensored,
Human learning and wild nature partnered.
But other children did not like his coarse hair,
And thought his shyness with them very quare.
Those who teased him, found something odd, peculiar,
Something frightening, and something wary, there;
In the flash of his eyes and in his stare.
To try it all alone, they would not dare.
But into his brief childhood of a sudden
There came a grief, both crushing and leaden.
Juan Darien was a year beyond eleven,
When his Mother suddenly was stricken.

MOTHER. Oh my son! Oh my beautiful one!
Oh child whose life has hardly just begun.
I fear I shall not see it done,
Because my life's thread has been spun,
And cannot be further outrun.
This fever has left me undone!

(MR. BONES dances with her and with JUAN DARIEN but eventually spins off the boy)

JUAN DARIEN. Mother! Do not leave me now!
Mother! Put your hand upon my brow!
Mother, I do not know how
To make my way with pen, or with plow!
I know not what life will allow,
To be a man I am not ready now.

(MR. BONES dances off stage with the MOTHER and onstage come MOURNERS carrying a coffin. A PALLBEARER speaks to JUAN DARIEN.)

PALLBEARER. Come my son, follow somberly the casket!
Leave all things of childish profit.
Pleasures here must be forfeit,
Times of grief are in surfeit.
Put on long pants, and a mourner's jacket,
Let your tears splash as down from a faucet,
'Till your eyes are as red as a sunset.
Hold not grief fast, or in private,
Let it pour forth like a mountain freshet!
Let there nothing be seen that is counterfeit,
But what speaks of the heart's great plummet.

(JUAN DARIEN joins the MOURNERS and follows the casket which leaves the stage.)

STORYTELLER. Thereafter came our young man palely,
To the grave of his dear Mother daily,
But still always somber, never gaily.
He stopped attending the school down in the valley,
He stopped, too, attending the church psalmody,
Withdrew to his own threnody;
Neither the night, nor day, had other melody.
But, slowly, haltingly, resignedly,
Did he dully, and then more purposefully,
Tear self away from the cairn;

Knowing he must either join her therein,
Or find a way to live on the mountain.
Find something to stanch the awful toxin!
And as he was pondering his plight,
There came, one evening, at twilight,
The sound of symbols and horns to excite
The mind of even the most sober acolyte,
Releasing in his soul the hidden Jacobin;
Attracting him like a moth to the light,
Raising in him a hearty appetite,
To visit the 'Big Top's' joys and delight,
To visit them – that very night!

CIRCUS BARKER. Come! Come one, come all to the Show!
We have some animals here from the Congo,
And acrobats with us from Moscow!
It will cost less than a *peso!*
This speech is not grand,
It gives you only a small window
Upon what is here on hand!
Young man why are you so slow
To reach in your pocket for *dinero?*
From your troubles it will be a godsend!

JUAN DARIEN. Sir, I am but a poor boy,
And I have no funds to employ!
But I can work if you need help,
More roustabouts, or a day boy.

CIRCUS BARKER. We don't need any *gauchos,*
Nor any young virtuosos.
Speak to people in the sideshows
To see if they need such fellows.

STORYTELLER. Juan Darien did as he was told,
But received a head shake at each threshold,
And nothing to put into his billfold;
And from some, there was even a scold!

At last he came to the veiled household
Of the glittering trapeze artist,
A rare and gifted aerialist,
Who also was a sensualist,
And no man left her presence still unnoticed,
Though married to the knife-throwing soloist.

TRAPEZE ARTIST. Come into my tent young man!
Are you a member of our clan?
Or, are you just here as a fan?
No matter…No…for you're a man!
Come in and sit on this divan!
Think you that I'm a courtesan?
Ah, no! No! No! Not marzipan.
Tell me about *you* partisan!

JUAN DARIEN. About me? Me? Well, I…don't know…
What is there to say about me?
I am light as a sparrow
Not imposing like a great tree!
I am not much, shall I go?

TRAPEZE ARTIST. Ah, ha ha ha my youthful scarecrow
You are a fine *caballero!*
No no please stay! Do not go!
Tell me, my modest Marco Polo,
Where's your home, your family?
Your Father? And poor Mother, also?

JUAN DARIEN. They are dead. For my beloved Mother was
a widow;
Then she died, a mere shadow,
From a fever that came through;
And left me in the deepest sorrow.

TRAPEZE ARTIST. Come close to me and let me hug you!
This is very, well, impromptu!
Though perhaps a kiss is overdue,
Would a kiss on those sweet lips be undue?

(Her husband the **KNIFE THROWER** *suddenly appears)*

KNIFE THROWER. So! What is this a rendezvous?
Another member of your retinue?
And pray tell young man, who are you?
Be quick now or else I shall strew
Your parts around this circus camp!
Now don't deny an *amor doux!*
And you, wife, are no ingenue!

TRAPEZE ARTIST. Oh, husband stop! I am no tramp!
You certainly do misconstrue
A thing that I now rue.
'Twas nothing more than charity,
To comfort this boy as you would have too.
But I will bid him here farewell
If you think it an impropriety.

KNIFE THROWER. Think you that I have not a clue?
That I cannot tell the false from true?
That I cannot see things are quite askew?
That I must not this, with force, subdue?
Lest it send all of us to hell!
This lesson is much overdue!
Wife, you shall have a front row view,
As my knife makes a bloody stew
Of this young cockatoo
Who'd, from here, now me expel.

JUAN DARIEN. Sir, I did not mean any harm!
Why do you take such quick alarm?
Please, good Sir, please, try to be calm!
What is it that is in your palm?
Wouldn't killing me not cause a qualm?

KNIFE THROWER. For me, from this, there is no balm!
You should have stayed upon your farm!
Now say the rosary...or else a psalm.

(Moves toward **JUAN DARIEN** *with his knife.* **JUAN DARIEN** *runs out of the tent with the* **KNIFE THROWER** *following.* **JUAN DARIEN** *makes his escape in the darkness.)*

JUAN DARIEN. It is too late to travel back.
  Perhaps there is a closer place,
  Blind to that man, that maniac,
  With his vengeful and angry face.
  Perhaps I could find a safe haystack…

  (suddenly the **KNIFE THROWER** *appears again and* **JUAN DARIEN** *flees, coming to the wild animal cages)*

  That madman will follow my track
  Until he finds me, or 'til I come back.
  Where can I hide this bony sack?
  Where can I lie free from attack?
  I'm caught here in a cul de sac
  Unless I enter this strange shack.

  (The **KNIFE THROWER** *appears at the end of the cul de sac and* **JUAN DARIEN** *disappears entering the tiger cage.)*

STORYTELLER. To the eye of man did he disappear;
  But to the tiger's eyes that night appear!
  Only they could the silent footsteps hear
  While growling out a grudging "welcome" clear,
  To a prodigal native of their lair.
  But in the morning came the trainer
  To look upon his feared charges there!

ANIMAL TRAINER. What's this? What have we here?
  It's something strange…yes something queer!
  A boy with tigers as a peer!
  Is he asleep or…*dead,* I fear!
  For beasts like these I shed no tear.
  Without my gun and whip to sear
  Their souls, and make them cower here,

They would have killed me came I *that* near!

STORYTELLER. The Trainer was so much amazed.
He went to town and there asked
Those he met: Whose son could be unfazed,
To sleep with wild animals, unless the boy was crazed?
The mayor said no children raised
In his town could have been so crosswaysed.
Perhaps an evil spirit, one unpraised,
Had stolen from the village a child and replaced
Him with an animal, false human-faced.
They both agreed it must be traced,
For, elsewise, human kind might be debased,
By beast, in human form carapaced.
Or, worse still, the villagers, with trust misplaced,
Could, by claw and tooth, from this world become displaced.

MAYOR. We'll hold a contest here,
Of all the school boys, far and near,
And ask them to imagine the space that
A feline predator holds dear.
And in their answers will inhere,
In *one*, the dreaded tiger's peer.
Then, strike we shall with rod and spear,
Lest it survive another year,
And haunt town and the jungle with a leer.

STORYTELLER. So they assembled children there;
And set for one a secret snare.
Of it, Juan Darien was not aware,
And he approached the match without a care.
But, the mayor now was within *his* lair
And looking close for something quaire,
Weighed every answer in his chair,
To catch a devil in mid air!

MAYOR. Children, I would like each of you,

In many words, or maybe few,
Of the jungle to give your view,
As those close to it best can do.
To him, with description most true,
There'll be a special prize or two.
But I stop there, lest I give a clue,
And so, without more ado,
Let's see what each of you can do.
You, down there, please come here onto
This platform for an interview.
Give us your name, make your debut!

CHILD 1. My name is José, if you please,
And I should win this prize with ease.
The jungle is full of tall trees,
And vines twined like dense helices,
And many birds and chickadees,
And beasts of different known species.
Sir, I hope I did not displease!

MAYOR. What you say, we have heard before.
We are here looking still for something more,
For something not the common store,
But you did well, with bookish lore!
And we commend you and your
Teacher, for his discipline and vigor.
Please send up the next young *señor*.

(**CHILD 1** *leaves and* **CHILD 2** *comes up*)

Son, let's see how you shall score
With this task, this perplexing chore.

CHILD 2. You say that you want something more
Than what José gave you before.
Then I shall tell you of seed and spore
That causes all of the jungle floor
To bloom so densely with flowers galore
In every shade and deepest color.

Or would you like to hear me "caw"
Like the birds that flying soar
Above the tree tops, past the maw
Of all below that screech and roar.

STORYTELLER. And so it went 'till all save one
Had there been questioned and were done.
And yet there still had been none
Who in this strange contest had won!

ANIMAL TRAINER. If I am not in error, Sir,
There is the one who did prefer
To sleep close by the tiger's fur,
To which I did before refer.
Nor did those beasts around him stir.
He was one of them I infer.
And not only was that his milieu,
But his eyes are yellowish, that's *sure*.

MAYOR. That is the boy Juan Darien,
Whose Mother was late overtaken
By Death, if I'm not mistaken.
She was, by a fever, stricken;
But he survived, and did not sicken.
Perhaps, of woman, once, he did not quicken;
But by spirits here was bidden,
And, in him our harm was hidden!
We shall see if he remains unshaken,
When, in him, the jungle we awaken.
Juan Darien, come…it's your turn
To see if you will be the one to earn
The prize, and for us to learn
Who is the best, before we must adjourn.

(**JUAN DARIEN** *comes upon the platform*)
What can *you* in the jungle here discern!

JUAN DARIEN. Most of what I know was said before,
About the trees and birds and so,
All of that I could but underscore!

MAYOR. Is there not still anything more?

JUAN DARIEN. No Sir, that is what I was taught.
   I do not know what more is sought;
   And I have given it much thought.

MAYOR. Let us try this. Close tight your eyes!
   And do not try to be so wise,
   But tell us, please, what does arise,
   About which you'd extemporize.
   Can you, please, simply summarize?

   (**JUAN DARIEN** *closes his eyes.*)

JUAN DARIEN. I see nothing I recognize.

MAYOR. But soon you will. Please scrutinize
   What it is and, then, verbalize.
   Tell us what does materialize.
   First, let us together hypothesize:
   That it is dark, before sunrise,
   And you have just eaten, somewise,
   And a stream crosses your path slantwise,
   And you're parched and realize
   That you must drink or agonize
   With thirst. What do you visualize?

JUAN DARIEN. *(shivers and speaks in a low voice)* I see rocks
   and a bending branch go by
   And the soft ground, and dead leaves lie
   Upon the rocks and putrefy...

MAYOR. One moment please...the rocks... how high?

JUAN DARIEN. They graze my ears as I pass by,
   Though on the soft ground they do lie.
   And the leaves tremble when I sigh.
   And I feel the dampness on my...
   (stops)

MAYOR. Do tell us, *where?* Please! Specify!

JUAN DARIEN. The dampness is on my...my *whiskers!*

(His eyes open wide.)

Has my tongue joined with tricksters?
Have all my senses gone awry?
My throat is *suddenly* quite dry!
All that I spoke…I should deny!
Full now awake, I needs must fly?

MAYOR. *(to the* **ANIMAL TRAINER***)* It is clear, Juan Darien
must die!
He is a spirit from the jungle nigh,
Perhaps a dread tiger, who must not ply
The streets of this place, where I try
To guard the populace close by.
But with his death the people need comply,
They must be swayed though, bye and bye.

ANIMAL TRAINER. He was the one who did sleep
With the tigers, and was not shy
And now I think I know why.

CHILDREN. *(laughing)* Juan Darien you have much gall,
To claim whiskers where you have none at all.
Your face is as smooth as a cannonball.

MAYOR. Children, the one whom you call,
With light hearted teasing and all,
Has a secret that would much appall
Everyone here, for what could befall
This town, if we don't it forestall.
For in his eyes there is a wall,
And there behind it is the squall
Of a tiger's fury that can maul
An older person with a shawl,
Or else an infant just starting to crawl,
And even the school child whose scrawl
Is found upon the blackboard wall.

CHILDREN. Juan Darien is a wild tiger? No!
But the mayor speaks, and he says it's so!

  But is it so? How can we know?
  Must we take it on his say so?

ANIMAL TRAINER. If he is a fierce tiger then he'll show
  A fear of the whip. *That* is how!
  So "Mister Tiger" here's a blow!

JUAN DARIEN. Where is the pity? What does he sow?

CHILDREN. There is a stripe…Let the blood flow!
  Let he who was haughty, eat crow!
  Let *all* of the proud, be laid low!
  Juan Darien, the tiger, must go!
  Hit him once again, Sir, with a blow!

MAYOR. Ah, children, now that you know,
  I trust that you will join in the dance!
  I praise you all, and say "Bravo"!
  Find a stick or lash and then follow!
  Bring your Fathers from their wheelbarrow,
  The Trainer here has broken our trance,
  And we must not wait until tomorrow.

JUAN DARIEN. This is madness, what a sorrow,
  The pain pierces the bone to the marrow!

STORYTELLER. All the children followed perfectly their
  elders,
  And the elders followed their heirs.
  Upon Juan Darien there came,
  Blow after blow much the same,
  Until his flesh bore the stripes of a tiger,
  And his heart felt grief sharper than vinegar.
  They pursued him, mercilessly, down the street,
  Until he stumbled, and fell, in retreat.
  Then, they seized him, and tied him to a wheel,
  That further stretched out the ordeal;
  For it was part of a fireworks display,
  That spun out fire and sparks into a spray,
  And burned flesh on its way to the ground,

As the wheel turned round and around.
Finally, when faint and near death,
With little left of life or breath,
They cut him down and left him for dead,
By the edge of the jungle. They said
He should die far away from men's graves
Far from all our human enclaves.
All through the night he did groan,
And for death alone did he moan,
'Til just before the break of the day,
When the snake came again, much in dismay.

SNAKE. Not twice shall man do such harm to you,
Without suffering what now is their due.
Take yourself deep into the heart of the jungle,
And I will give you these herbs in a bundle
And you shall change into what all men fear,
And all that is human will remain here.

STORYTELLER. So Juan Darien crawled far away,
He left behind the light, and the day,
Retreating to the deepest part, so cool and so dark,
Far from the hand of man, and his mark.
There, with time and with the snake's gift,
His body healed and spirits did lift.
But his eyes now glowed in the night,
Like the tigers, and his skin gave a fright,
For the flesh healed but the scars still remained,
And where they were, the flesh was stained
The color an inky dark brown,
And between was the shade of a tropic sundown.
The hair on his head and his body
Grew, and gave a true bona fide,
Of the color of the body underneath.
And, too, grew his nails and his teeth,
And whiskers out from the side of his jowl,

That allowed him to hunt and to prowl
In the night, whether moonlit or black,
And to keep to the trail or the track.
But as he grew stronger he thought
Of the dread Trainer and the things he'd wrought.
Then, he decided that he should return,
To the town, so that the people might learn
The harvest of the seeds they'd sown;
Of what they had done to their own.
So one day he left the dark heart
Of the deep jungle, where he did start out;
And climbing a tree on an urge
He bided his time like a scourge.
Hid safe away among the leaves,
High over the sugar cane sheaves.
Until he viewed what he had come after
And his heart filled with savage laughter.
When he saw the gun and vicious whip,
He loosed, from the tree, his tight grip,
And leapt on the man in his pride,
And knocked him down on his side.
The lash and the revolver were lost,
As the man saw tiger and ghost,
Of the Juan Darien he had left for dead;
Which now the tiger had largely shed.
But in his tiger form he still recalled
How to tie rope, how to sear and to scald.
And he bound the Trainer to the cane,
For he was now the Trainer's suzerain.
And then he lit the cane with a match,
And watched it burn like dry thatch.

ANIMAL TRAINER. Please, Juan Darien, cut me down!
Don't leave me here to die alone!

STORYTELLER. Juan Darien heard, but he turned away,

For he repaid what he'd come to repay.
Before his ties to the town could be severed,
He went to his Mother's grave and endeavored
To bid her good bye, and to say, in his pain,
That her love, and her care, were not in vain.
But from his throat came only a growl,
While in his heart was a desperate howl.
For he had lost the power of human speech,
The power to explain, the power to beseech.
Then scratching, on his side, deeply, a scar
He wrote in blood on the tomb, to her star,
"Juan Darien lies here too, Mother"!
And he returned to the deep jungle forever.

So, *Señor*, is my account here finished';
Their worlds and realm, save me, all vanished'!
I have their story here told you;
And, or it *live*, you must now tell it too!

THE END

www.ingramcontent.com/pod-product-compliance
Lightning Source LLC
Chambersburg PA
CBHW070422120726
47909CB00005B/1763